Invitations to Personal Reading
Curriculum Foundation Classroom Library
Scott, Foresman and Company

Books to Read Aloud	
The Big Golden Book of Poetry	edited by Jane Werner
Finders Keepers	Will and Nicolas
Little Frightened Tiger	Golden MacDonald
The Man Who Didn't Wash His Dishes	Phyllis Krasilovsky
The Old Woman and Her Pig	illustrated by Paul Galdone
Rosa-Too-Little	Sue Felt
Six Foolish Fishermen	retold by Benjamin Elkin
The Three Billy Goats Gruff	P. C. Asbjørnsen and J. E. Moe
Umbrella	Taro Yashima
Where Does the Butterfly Go When It Rains	May Garelick

Books to Enrich the Content Fields	
The Big Book of Real Fire Engines	illustrated by George Zaffo
The Listening Walk	Paul Showers
One Snail and Me	Emilie McLeod
The Sky Was Blue	Charlotte Zolotow
What Is A Turtle	Gene Darby

Books for Independent Reading	
Belling the Cat and Other Stories	retold by Leland Jacobs
Big Talk	Miriam Schlein
Cowboy Small	Lois Lenski
Gertie the Duck	Nicholas Georgiady and Louis Romano
Indian Two Feet and His Horse	Margaret Friskey
Josie and the Snow	Helen Buckley
Karen's Opposites	A. and M. Provensen
Millions and Millions and Millions!	Louis Slobodkin
Nothing but Cats, Cats, Cats	Grace Skaar
Robins and Rabbits	John Hawkinson

THE SKY WAS BLUE

THE SKY

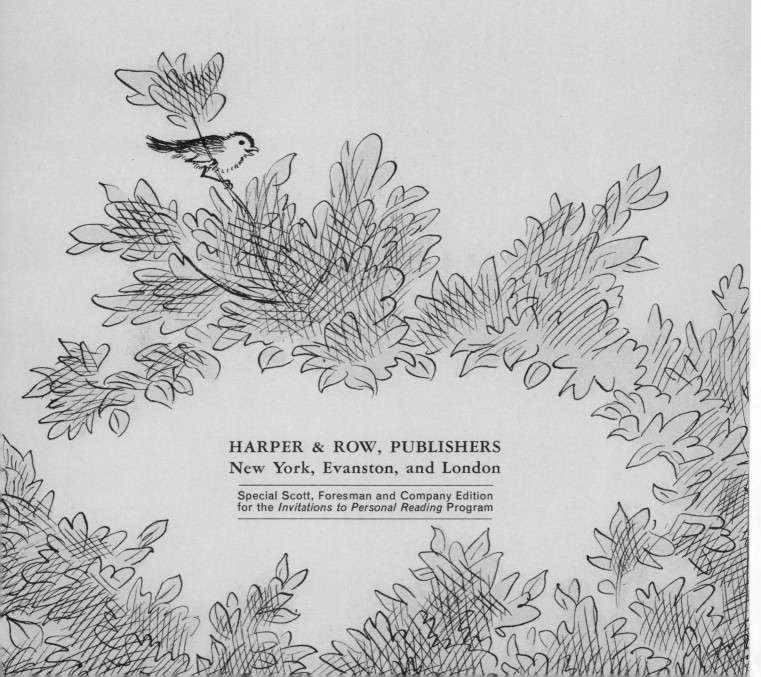

HARPER & ROW, PUBLISHERS
New York, Evanston, and London

Special Scott, Foresman and Company Edition
for the *Invitations to Personal Reading* Program

WAS BLUE

by Charlotte Zolotow
Pictures by Garth Williams

THE SKY WAS BLUE

To Harriet Kahnweiler
and her daughters and her granddaughters

"Is this you?" said the little girl to her mother.

The little girl was looking at a picture

in the family album of another little girl.

The little girl in the picture and the little girl looking

at the picture both had long black hair.

But the little girl in the picture

wore hers tied back with a bow.

"Yes, that's a picture of me

when I was just as old as you

are now," said the little girl's mother.

"What funny clothes," the little girl said.

"I thought they were pretty," said her mother, "for when I was little,

I wore a dress like this.

I had a doll like this.

We had a car like this.

And I lived in a house like this."

"What was it like? How did you feel?"

the little girl asked.

"Oh," said her mother, "I felt the way you feel.

Important things will always be the same:

The sky was blue,

grass was green,

snow was white and cold,

the sun was warm and yellow,

just as they all are now.

"When I went to bed,

I wanted my mother to hug me before she turned off the light.

And when I lay in bed,

the room was dark,

the clocks ticked,

the grown-ups talked downstairs,

and I could hear the wind in the trees outside, just as you do now."

The little girl turned another page in the picture album.

"How was it for *your* mother?" she asked.

"Grandmother?"

"Yes."

"Oh," said the little girl's mother. "When she was little, she wore a dress like this:

She had a doll like this:

They rode in a car like this:

And she lived in a house like this."

"What was it like? How did she feel?" the little girl asked.

"Oh," said her mother, "the way you feel.

The sky was blue,

grass was green,

snow was white and cold,

the sun was warm and yellow,

just as they all are now.

"When she went to bed, she wanted her mother to hug her

before she turned off the light.

And when she lay in bed,

the room was dark,

the clocks ticked,

the grown-ups talked downstairs,

and she could hear the wind in the trees outside, just as you do now."

The little girl turned another page

in the picture album.

"And *her* mother?" she asked.

"Your great-grandmother?"

"Yes," said the little girl.

"Oh," said the little girl's mother,

"when she was little,

she wore a dress like this.   And a hat like this.

She had a doll like this.

When she went visiting, she rode in a carriage with a horse like this.

And she lived in a house like this."

"What was it like? How did she feel?" the little girl asked.

"Oh," said her mother, "the way you feel.

The sky was blue,

grass was green,

snow was white and cold,

the sun was warm and yellow,

just as they all are now.

"When she went to bed, she wanted her mother to hug her before

she blew out the candle. And when she lay in bed,

the room was dark,

the clocks ticked,

the grown-ups talked downstairs,

the stars shone in the sky,

and she could hear the wind in the trees outside, just as you do now."

The little girl closed the photograph album

and leaned against her mother.

"Is that all?" said the little girl.

"No," said her mother.

"Someday, you'll be showing your picture to your little girl,

and you will be telling her that...

the sky will always be blue.

Grass will always be green.

Snow will always be white and cold.

The sun will always be warm and yellow

And then," said her mother,